P9-CQQ-116

12-06-06

6-1-05

Flatfoot Fox

and the Case of the Missing Eye

Flatfoot Fox

and the Case of the Missing Eye

ETH CLIFFORD

Illustrated by Brian Lies

Houghton Mifflin Company

Boston 1990

1-2
c.1

For all the dedicated teachers
and librarians who spark
the joy of reading
in children—E.C.

For my parents—B.L.

Text copyright © 1990 by Eth Clifford Rosenberg
Illustrations copyright © 1990 by Brian Lies

All rights reserved. For information about permission to reproduce selections from this book, write to Permissions, Houghton Mifflin Company, 2 Park Street, Boston, Massachusetts 02108.

Library of Congress Cataloging-in-Publication Data

Clifford, Eth, date.
    Flatfoot Fox and the case of the missing eye / Eth Clifford ;
illustrations by Brian Lies.
        p.   cm.
    Summary: Detective Fox uncovers the thief who stole Fat Cat's glass eye.
    ISBN 0-395-51945-4
    [1. Mystery and detective stories. 2. Foxes—Fiction.
3. Animals—Fiction.] I. Lies, Brian, ill. II. Title.
PZ7.C62214F1   1990
[Fic]—dc20   89-26862
                CIP
                AC

Printed in the United States of America

HOR 10 9 8 7 6 5 4 3 2 1

CHICAGO HEIGHTS FREE PUBLIC LIBRARY

Contents

10-31-91   1356   12.95

1.
Fat Cat

"I am the smartest detective in the whole world," said Flatfoot Fox.

"I know," said Secretary Bird. "It says so on the door. It says *Flatfoot Fox, the Smartest Detective in the Whole World.* I've always wanted to ask you. Is that true? The smartest detective in the whole world?"

"Of course it's true. I put those words on the door myself," said Flatfoot Fox.

Just then there was a knock on the door.

"Come in," called Flatfoot Fox.

Fat Cat came in.

He had a patch over one eye. It was a big, black patch.

Fat Cat's other eye was a mean tiger eye, yellow, with a black dot in the middle.

Fat Cat was big. Fat Cat was mean. And Fat Cat was mad.

"Someone stole my eye. I want you to find it," Fat Cat told Flatfoot Fox.

"Your eye?" Secretary Bird asked. "Your eye is in your head."

"Not that eye. My glass eye," said Fat Cat.

"What color is it?" asked Flatfoot Fox.

"It must be a tiger eye," said Secretary Bird. "A yellow eye, with a black dot in the middle, just like your real eye."

"No," said Fat Cat. "I don't like tiger eyes. I like blue. My glass eye is a beautiful sky blue. And I want it back."

"Where was your glass eye the last time you looked?" Flatfoot Fox asked.

"In my eye cup, of course."

"When did you find out that your eye was missing?" Flatfoot Fox said.

"At my party. My birthday party. I put my eye

9

in my eye cup because I wanted to sing. You can't sing with a glass eye," said Fat Cat.

Secretary Bird was surprised. "Why not?"

"Because I sing loud. And I sing hard. I sang

H A P P Y

Happy Birthday to Me loud and hard. When I sing loud and hard, my glass eye pops out," said Fat Cat. "When I stopped singing, I looked in my eye cup. My eye was gone. Someone stole it."

"Who came to your party? Do you have a list?" asked Secretary Bird.

"I have a list of all the suspects," said Fat Cat.

"Suspects? What is a suspect?" Secretary Bird wanted to know.

Flatfoot Fox explained. "A suspect is someone who may be guilty. Or not be guilty."

"They are all guilty," Fat Cat shouted. "GUILTY! GUILTY! GUILTY!"

"How can they all be guilty?" asked Flatfoot Fox.

"They were angry because I ate the birthday cake before they came. And all the ice cream, too."

"You had a birthday party with no birthday cake? And no ice cream?" Flatfoot Fox was surprised. "Why?"

"Because they call me names. They say I am big and fat and mean," said Fat Cat.

"But you are big and fat and mean," said Secretary Bird.

"I know. But I do not like to hear it. Now I need a detective to find my eye. Can you find it?" asked Fat Cat.

"Of course," said Flatfoot Fox. "After all, I am the smartest detective in the whole world."

As soon as Fat Cat left, Flatfoot Fox told Secretary Bird, "I must talk to all the suspects. Who is first?"

Secretary Bird looked at the list. "The first one

is Really Ridiculous Rabbit. What a funny name. Why is he called Really Ridiculous Rabbit?"

"You will soon find out. Let's go," said Flatfoot Fox.

"Yes," said Secretary Bird. "Let's go."

2.
Really Ridiculous Rabbit

Flatfoot Fox and Secretary Bird found Really Ridiculous Rabbit in a garden. He was eating a carrot. When he saw them, he called out, "Want a carrot? They are really very good."

"No," said Flatfoot Fox. "I don't eat when I am on a case."

"What case?" asked Really Ridiculous Rabbit.

"The case of the missing eye," Flatfoot Fox explained. "Someone stole Fat Cat's eye."

"His I? That is really ridiculous," said Really Ridiculous Rabbit. "Why would anyone steal the letter *I*? If I stole a letter, I would steal a *Q*. A *Q* has a tail. I have a tail. Tails are wonderful."

"How ridiculous you are," said Flatfoot Fox.

17

"Someone has stolen Fat Cat's glass eye. You were at the birthday party. So you are a suspect."

"A suspect?" Really Ridiculous Rabbit asked. "Thank Q. How wonderful. I have never been a suspect before. What do I have to do?"

"You have to give back the glass eye if you stole it," Secretary Bird said.

"That is really ridiculous," said Really Ridiculous Rabbit. "If I stole it, why would I want to give it back?"

"I'm supposed to ask the questions," said Flatfoot Fox. "A detective always asks the questions. And I am the greatest detective in the whole world. Now, tell me. Did you see Fat Cat's glass eye when you were at the birthday party?"

"Yes. I saw it."

"What color was Fat Cat's eye?" Flatfoot Fox asked.

Really Ridiculous Rabbit looked surprised. "That is a really ridiculous question. Fat Cat's glass eye is like his real eye. It is a tiger eye, yellow, with a black dot in the middle. What a really ridiculous color for an eye. An eye should be pink. My eyes are pink. I have white fur. White fur and pink eyes are beautiful."

"I see," said Flatfoot Fox.

"What do you see?" asked Secretary Bird.

"I will tell you later," said Flatfoot Fox. "A detective never solves a mystery right away."

"That is really ridiculous," said Really Ridiculous Rabbit. "Why can't a detective solve a mystery right away?"

"Detectives don't answer questions. They ask them. Now," Flatfoot Fox told Secretary Bird. "We have to talk to our next suspect. Who is next on the list?"

"Picky Pig," said Secretary Bird.

"Thank Q for coming," said Really Ridiculous

Rabbit as Flatfoot Fox and Secretary Bird left. "Remember," he called after them. "Think pink!"

3.
Picky Pig

Picky Pig was in his pen. His mother was eating. His father was eating.

Picky Pig's mother stopped eating. She shouted at Picky Pig, "Picky. Picky. Picky. You have been picky since the day you were born. You are picky about where you sleep. You are picky about who will be your friends. Worst of all, you are picky about what you eat. You cannot go on being a picky eater. You must eat everything."

"You will never be a hog if you are a picky eater," his father shouted.

"Do I have to be a hog?" asked Picky Pig.

"Yes. First you must make a pig of yourself. Then you will turn into a hog."

"Picky Pig," Flatfoot Fox called. "I want to ask you some questions."

"What kind of questions?" asked Picky Pig. "I am very picky about the kind of questions I will answer."

Secretary Bird pecked Picky Pig. "You must answer Flatfoot Fox's questions, picky or not. Or I will peck you harder, like this."

Secretary Bird pecked Picky Pig again, to show him.

"Did you see Fat Cat's eye when you were at the birthday party?" Flatfoot Fox asked.

"Yes. I saw it."

24

"What color was Fat Cat's glass eye?"

"Don't you know?" asked Picky Pig. "The smartest detective in the whole world should know that. It was a tiger eye, yellow, with a black dot in the middle."

"Are you sure?" asked Flatfoot Fox.

"Of course. I would never want a tiger eye. Eyes should be brown. Like mud. I like mud, don't you?"

Picky Pig began to roll back and forth in a mud puddle.

"Mud is beautiful," he said. "Brown is beautiful."

"I see," said Flatfoot Fox.

"What do you see?" asked Secretary Bird.

"I will tell you later. When I have solved the mystery," said Flatfoot Fox. "Who is next on the list?"

"Greedy Goat," said Secretary Bird.

As Secretary Bird and Flatfoot Fox left, Picky Pig shouted after them, "Think mud!"

HOG HEAVEN
FEEDS

4.
Greedy Goat

"Look," said Secretary Bird. "There is Greedy Goat, at the top of the hill."

As soon as Flatfoot Fox and Secretary Bird came near him, Greedy Goat asked, "Did you bring me some food?"

"Why should we bring you food?" asked Secretary Bird.

"Because I am hungry. H-U-N-G-R-Y!"

Greedy Goat looked at a big clock he wore around his neck. "I have not had food for one whole hour."

He looked all around. "There is nothing left on this hill. I wish I had some cans. Munchy, crunchy cans. I dream about munchy, crunchy cans at

29

CHICAGO HEIGHTS FREE PUBLIC LIBRARY

night. I dream about munchy, crunchy cans in the day."

"We are not here to talk about food," said Flat-foot Fox.

Greedy Goat was surprised, "But what else is there to talk about? When I am not eating, I think about eating. And when I think about eating, I talk about eating. And that makes me very hungry."

"Stop!" Secretary Bird shouted. "Stop talking and listen."

"What did you do at Fat Cat's birthday party?" asked Flatfoot Fox.

"There was nothing to do. There was no birthday cake and no ice cream. Fat Cat ate it all before we came to the party. All that was left were paper cups and paper plates. They were tasty," said Greedy Goat.

"Did you eat Fat Cat's glass eye?"

"No! I only looked at it. I did not eat it. You think I eat everything in sight."

"But you do eat everything in sight," said Secretary Bird.

"I wouldn't eat something that was looking at me," said Greedy Goat.

"What color was the eye?" asked Flatfoot Fox.

"It was a mean tiger eye, yellow, with a black dot in the middle, of course," said Greedy Goat.

"I see," said Flatfoot Fox.

"What do you see?" asked Secretary Bird. "I don't see anything."

"That is because I am the detective, and I know when I am told a lie or the truth," said Flatfoot Fox.

"Did Really Ridiculous Rabbit lie?"

"Yes," said Flatfoot Fox.

"And Picky Pig? And Greedy Goat?"

"Of course," said Flatfoot Fox. "Now it is time to find the next suspect on the list."

As they left, Greedy Goat shouted after them, "Think f-o-o-d!"

5.
Snake-in-the-Grass

"The next suspect is Snake-in-the-Grass," said Secretary Bird. "He will not be easy to see. He will not be easy to hear. How will we find him?"

"You will not have to find me. I have found you," said a voice. The voice came from close by. It was the voice of Snake-in-the-Grass. "I was sleeping. You woke me up."

Secretary Bird looked all around. "Where are you?"

"I am right near your feet."

Secretary Bird jumped back. "You scared me. Come out where we can see you."

So Snake-in-the-Grass slid up a tree. He slid

round and round the tree. "Why did you wake me up?"

"I must ask you some questions," said Flatfoot Fox.

"Go away. I do not answer questions," said Snake-in-the-Grass.

"My questions are important," said Flatfoot Fox. "He is falling asleep again," Flatfoot Fox told Secretary Bird.

Secretary Bird pecked Snake-in-the-Grass hard. He pecked until Snake-in-the-Grass woke up.

"Did you see Fat Cat's glass eye when you were at his party?" Flatfoot Fox asked.

"Glass eye? What glass eye?" asked Snake-in-the-Grass. "What color was it?"

Flatfoot Fox smiled. "Why it was a tiger eye, of course. Yellow, with a black dot in the middle."

"It was not!" Snake-in-the-Grass shouted. "It was sky blue. A beautiful sky blue. It was the most beautiful sky blue eye I have ever seen."

"Aha!" Flatfoot Fox said. "YOU STOLE FAT CAT'S EYE!"

"No fair," said Snake-in-the-Grass. "You tricked me."

"Why did you steal the glass eye?"

"Fat Cat has one good eye. A mean tiger eye,

with a black dot in the middle. He doesn't need his glass eye. I need that eye."

"What for?" asked Secretary Bird.

"What are you going to do with it?" Flatfoot Fox asked.

"I am a long snake. When I move, I can see where I am going. But I cannot see where I have been. My tail is too far from my head. Now, with Fat Cat's glass eye, I will be able to see where I have been."

Snake-in-the-Grass came down from the tree. He stretched from head to tail.

Now Flatfoot Fox and Secretary Bird saw Fat Cat's glass eye. It was stuck on the tip of the snake's tail.

Secretary Bird pecked the glass eye from the tail and gave it to Flatfoot Fox.

"What a snake-in-the-grass you are!" shouted Secretary Bird.

"And not a very smart one," said Flatfoot Fox. "Don't you know you can't see with a glass eye?"

"You don't know until you try," said Snake-in-the-Grass. He slid up the tree. Then he shouted down at them, "Fat Cat is mean. I am mean, too. Think mean!" he called after them as they left.

6.
A Knock on the Door

"I really am the smartest detective in the whole world," said Flatfoot Fox. "I found the one who stole Fat Cat's eye. I gave the eye back to Fat Cat. The case of the missing eye is closed."

"Yes," said Secretary Bird. "But you never told me how you solved the mystery. You always said you would tell me later. Is it later now?"

"Yes," said Flatfoot Fox. "Do you remember that I said Really Ridiculous Rabbit lied? And Picky Pig? And Greedy Goat?"

"I remember. But how did you know they lied?" asked Secretary Bird.

"Do you remember that I asked each of them the color of the glass eye?"

"I remember," said Secretary Bird.

"And what did all the suspects say?"

Secretary Bird thought and thought. Then he thought some more.

"I know," he said at last. "They all said it was a tiger eye, yellow, with a black dot in the middle."

"That was the wrong answer. The glass eye was sky blue. A beautiful sky blue. They all said they saw the eye at the birthday party. But they said it was a tiger eye. So they all lied when they said they saw it," said Flatfoot Fox.

"How clever you are," said Secretary Bird. "But

one of them could have taken the eye anyway."

"No," said Flatfoot Fox. "Really Ridiculous Rabbit only likes pink eyes. Picky Pig only likes brown eyes, like mud. Greedy Goat will not take anything he can't eat."

"Then why did they lie if they didn't take the eye?" Secretary Bird wondered.

"They were suspects. Suspects always lie to a detective. If they didn't, there wouldn't be a mystery."

"Oh," said Secretary Bird. "And if there wasn't a mystery, you couldn't solve it. And you couldn't be

a detective anymore. But how did you know Snake-in-the-Grass was guilty?"

"I tricked him into telling the truth. He was the only one who thought a sky blue eye is beautiful," said Flatfoot Fox with a big smile.

Just then there was a knock on the door.

"Who can that be?" asked Secretary Bird. He looked at the door.

Flatfoot Fox looked at the door.

"Who is there?" called Flatfoot Fox.

There was another knock on the door.

"Come in," Flatfoot Fox shouted. He smiled at Secretary Bird. "I wonder who it can be."

The door began to open slowly.

"It could be your next case," said Secretary Bird.

Flatfoot Fox watched to see who was opening the door.

"I wonder," said Flatfoot Fox. "I wonder if it will be as mysterious as the case of the missing eye."

j
2-3
c.1

CHICAGO HEIGHTS FREE PUBLIC LIBRARY

1-2

CHICAGO HEIGHTS FREE PUBLIC LIBRARY
3 1589 00113 4030

QJ, 99, 02, 08, 13,

j-CLIFFORD, ETH.   1-2-3
  Flatfoot fox and the case of the
  missing eye.
  c. 1

CHICAGO HEIGHTS FREE PUBLIC LIBRARY
15TH ST. & CHICAGO ROAD
CHICAGO HEIGHTS, ILL.
60411
PHONE: (708) 754-0323